The Balloon in the Tree

and The Very Strange Pool

illustrated by
Rene Cloke

AWARD PUBLICATIONS LIMITED

The Balloon
in the Tree

Once there was a pixie called Winks who had a fine, big, blue balloon. He had got it at a party and he was very proud of it indeed. It had a long string, and Winks took it with him wherever he went.

One day he went out with his balloon, and the wind blew so hard that it tugged the string out of Winks's hand. The balloon went up into the air and flew straight into a tall tree. There it stuck, high up on a branch, wobbling a little whenever the wind blew.

'Oh!' cried Winks in dismay. 'Come down, balloon! How silly you look up there! Come down.'

The balloon took no notice of Winks at all. It just sat up in the tree and wobbled. Winks wondered if he could climb the tree and fetch it down. But it was much too hard a tree to climb.

'Oh dear! I can't lose my lovely balloon!' said Winks. 'I really can't. I wonder what I can do to get it down.'

THE BALLOON IN THE TREE

Now just then who should come by but Mr Hobble with his stick. Winks ran up to him.

'Mr Hobble! Give me your stick for a minute! I want to get my balloon down.'

He snatched away Mr Hobble's stick and ran back to the tree. But the stick wouldn't reach even halfway to the balloon. So Winks threw the stick up into the tree, hoping to move the balloon and make it float down.

But alas! The stick flew up and stayed in the tree. Its curved handle hung on a branch and there the stick swung, just by the balloon. Mr Hobble was very angry indeed.

'How dare you do that!' he cried. 'You wicked pixie! If you don't get my stick down for me I will shake you till your teeth rattle like dice!'

THE BALLOON IN THE TREE

Winks was frightened. Then he saw Miss Sally Simple coming along with a fine, fat, red umbrella. He ran up to her.

'Sally Simple! Let me have your umbrella for a minute. Mr Hobble's stick is stuck up in the tree and I must get it down for him.'

He snatched at Sally's umbrella and ran
back to the tree. He sent the umbrella
flying up into the branches to hit the stick
down – but alas, it too stuck up in the
tree, swinging by its handle from a high
branch!

Well, if Mr Hobble was angry, Sally
Simple was even angrier.

She shook Winks hard and cried, 'If you don't climb up that tree and get down my umbrella I'll drop you, *splash*! into that pond over there!'

Winks began to cry. This was dreadful. Whatever was he to do?

Then he saw Mr Dig the gardener coming along, his spade over his shoulder. He ran up to him.

'Mr Dig, dear Mr Dig, lend me your spade to get down Sally Simple's umbrella from that tree!' he cried.

Before Mr Dig could say yes or no, Winks had snatched the spade from him and had run back to the tree. Up went the spade – *crash*! into the tree. It didn't hit the stick. It didn't hit the umbrella. It just broke two or three small branches – and then stayed high up in the tree, looking very peculiar there along with the balloon, the stick, and the umbrella!

'Now, look here, Winks, what in the wide world do you think you are doing?' cried Mr Dig angrily. 'Are you making that tree into a Christmas tree and hanging it with presents for somebody – because that is what it is beginning to look like! Now just you get my spade for me, or I'll put you into that holly bush over there!'

Well, Mr Dig looked so fierce that Winks began to shiver and shake. He couldn't think *what* to do. And then he saw little Mrs Dot coming with her tennis-racket. She was on her way to a party. He ran up to her at once.

'Mrs Dot, be a pet and lend me your racket for a minute. I want to get Mr Dig's spade down from that tree. It's stuck up there.'

'But how did it get up there?' asked Mrs Dot in great surprise. 'My goodness – look at the things up there! Whatever's happened? Winks, you are not to throw my racket up into that tree. I forbid you to!'

But the racket had already gone! And there it stuck, of course, looking just as silly as all the other things. Mrs Dot was so angry that she went as red as the bow on her dress.

'Mr Dig! Sally Simple! Mr Hobble! How can you stand there and let Winks do these things? Here, take hold of one of his arms, Mr Dig. We'll send him up into the tree to fetch down our things! Now then, are you ready? One – two – three – and *up* he goes!'

And up Winks went! My goodness, what a shock he got! He flew through the air right up into the tree and landed just by the spade. He wept bitterly and pushed the spade off the branch. It fell down to the ground and Mr Dig went off with it.

Then Winks pushed down Sally's umbrella. She went off with that. Next, Mr Hobble's stick fell down, and after that Mrs Dot's racket. The two of them walked off, talking loudly about people who threw things up into trees.

THE BALLOON IN THE TREE

'Hi! Come back and help me down!' yelled Winks, who knew quite well that he couldn't climb down by himself. But nobody paid the least attention to him and soon he was quite alone up in the tree. The wind came to have a look at him – and it blew the balloon right out of the tree! Winks saw it flying down, down, down – and he saw the sandy rabbit come out of his hole to have a look at it.

THE BALLOON IN THE TREE

He saw the sandy rabbit nibble it to see if it tasted good – and he heard a loud *POP*! as the balloon burst into bits! The sandy rabbit turned and fled for his life and didn't come out of his hole again for two days.

'There goes my balloon!' wept poor Winks. 'Oh, dear, what an unlucky fellow I am! Whenever shall I get down from this horrible tree? Perhaps I shall be here all my life long!'

Well, he won't be – but he'll have to stay there until the evening when Mr Dig comes back from his work and will get a ladder to help him down. Poor Winks – he won't throw things up into trees again for a very long time!

The Very Strange Pool

Now, once upon a time Shiny-One the gnome had to take a heavy mirror to Dame Pretty.

It was a very large looking-glass indeed, bigger than Shiny-One himself, so it made him puff and pant, as you can imagine.

When he got to the middle of Cuckoo Wood he felt that he really must have a rest. So he laid the mirror flat on the ground, with the bracken and grass peeping into it, and went to lean against a tree a little way off. And he fell fast asleep.

Now along that way came little Peep and Pry, the two pixies who lived at the edge of the wood. They were always peeping and prying into things that were no business of theirs – so you can guess they were most astonished to see a big, flat, shining thing in the middle of the wood!

'Look at that!' said Peep. 'A new pool!'

'A lovely shiny pool!' said Pry. They both ran to it – and indeed, the mirror did look exactly like a shining pool of clear water, for it reflected the grass, the bracken, the trees, and the sky, exactly as a sheet of water does.

'I wonder how a pool suddenly came to be here,' said Peep. 'It's really rather extraordinary. There was never one here before.'

'It hasn't been raining,' said Pry. 'I just can't understand it. Do you suppose it is a magic pool, Peep?'

'Yes – perhaps it is,' said Peep.

'Peep – shall we take a little drink from it, in case it's a wishing-pool?' whispered Pry.

'Well – do you think we'd better?' said Peep. 'Suppose it belongs to somebody?'

'They'll never know,' said naughty Pry. "Come on – let's scoop a little water up in our hands and drink it. We'll wish at the same time."

Peep put his hand down to the mirror – but, of course, all he felt was something hard, and not soft water! He stared in astonishment.

'The pool's frozen!' he said. 'Look – there's no water – only ice.'

'Well, that *shows* it's magic!' said Pry at once. 'That just shows it is! How could water freeze on a warm spring day like this? It's impossible.'

'I think you're right,' said Peep in excitement. 'Yes, I really think you are. A pool that is frozen hard on a warm day *must* be magic! Whoever it belongs to must have frozen it so that nobody could take a drink and wish.'

'Ah – but we can manage to trick the owner!' said Pry in a whisper. 'We can break the ice, Peep – and drink the water below! Can't we?'

'Of course!' said Peep. 'Come on – let's break it and drink quickly, before anyone comes.'

'So they took stones and banged the pool hard – *crack*! The mirror broke into little pieces – and to the pixies' great astonishment there was no water underneath!

'Stranger and stranger!' said Peep. 'I wish there was somebody we could tell this to.'

Then they saw Shiny-One the gnome, not very far off, just waking up. They ran to him.

'I say, there's a magic pool over there!'

'We knew it was magic because it was frozen hard.'

'So we cracked the ice to get a drink of the water underneath – but there wasn't any! Did you ever know such magic?'

'What nonsense are you talking?' said Shiny-One crossly. He knew Peep and Pry well and didn't like the way they poked their noses into things that had nothing to do with them. 'A magic pool – frozen on a day like this! Rubbish!'

Peep and Pry took him to the pool – and Shiny-One stared down in horror at his poor broken mirror.

'My mirror!' he said. 'The one I was selling to Dame Pretty. Look what you've done, with your silly interfering ways – smashed that beautiful big mirror! You bad pixies! How much money have you got in your pockets? You'll have to pay for that mirror.'

THE VERY STRANGE POOL

Peep and Pry tried to run away – but Shiny-One caught hold of them both. He turned them upside down and shook them well. All their money rolled out of their pockets.

'Thank you,' said Shiny-One, and he turned the pixies the right way up. 'Thank you! Just enough to pay for a new mirror, I think. Now run off before I think of chasing you all the way home.'

Peep and Pry ran off, crying. Shiny-One dug a hole with a stick and buried all the bits of broken mirror, so that nobody's feet would get cut.

As for Peep and Pry, they couldn't buy sweets for four weeks because all their money had gone – so maybe they won't go poking their noses about quite so much another time!

ISBN 0-86163-776-3

Text copyright Darrell Waters Limited
Illustrations copyright © 1995 Award Publications Limited

Enid Blyton's signature is a trademark of Darrell Waters Limited

First published 1946 by Sampson Low in
Enid Blyton's Holiday Book series

This edition first published 1995 by Award Publications Limited,
27 Longford Street, London NW1 3DZ

Printed in Italy